Deep in the Forest

Deep in the Forest

by Brinton Turkle

A Puffin Unicorn

Unicorn is a registered trademark of Dutton Children's Books

Library of Congress number 76-21691

ISBN 0-14-054745-2

Published in the United States by Dutton Children's Books
a division of Penguin Books USA Inc.

375 Hudson Street, New York, NY 10014

Editor: Ann Durell

Printed in Hong Kong by South China Printing Co.

First Unicorn Edition 1987   W

10 9 8 7 6 5